Ten Tiny Turtles

A Crazy Counting Book

Paul Cherrill

Copyright © 1995 by Paul Cherrill
First American edition 1995 published by
Ticknor & Fields Books for Young Readers
A Houghton Mifflin Company, 215 Park Avenue South,
New York, New York 10003.

First published in Great Britain by Methuen Childrens Books, an imprint of
Reed Consumer Books Ltd.
Manufactured in Hong Kong.

Library of Congress Cataloging-in-Publication Data

Cherrill, Paul,
    Ten Tiny Turtles / by Paul Cherrill. — 1st American ed.
p.   cm.
    Summary: All kinds of animals, from a water-squirting dog to ten
    tiny turtles in T-shirts, illustrate the numbers from one to ten.
                    ISBN 0-395-71250-5
        [1. Animals-Fiction. 2. Counting. 3. Stories in rhyme.]
                I. Title II. Title: 10 tiny turtles.
PZ8.3.C426TE 1995
[E]-dc20   94-19904
                                                    CIP
                                                    AC

Ten Tiny Turtles
A Crazy Counting Book

Paul Cherrill

Ticknor & Fields Books for Young Readers
New York 1995

1

One playful dog
squirting water
at the cat

2

Two rabbits dancing~
how about that

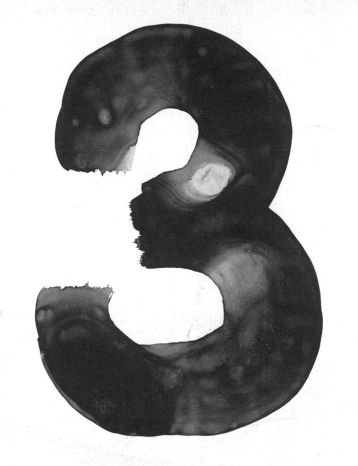

3

Three pies baked by
the rat dressed
for dinner

4

Four bottles of Pop for the chicken race winner

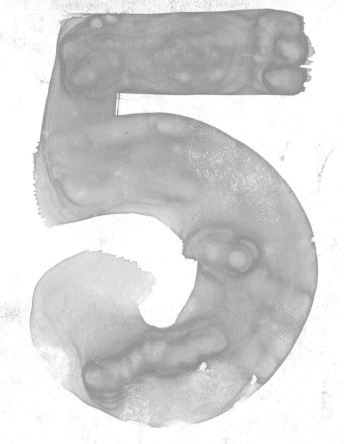

5

Five fluffy sheep
pretending to
be clouds

Six slim cats
standing tall and
looking proud

Seven slimy worms
wearing glasses
in the sun

Eight spotted fish
Playing hockey
just for fun

9

Nine noisy bees
for the fat toad
to catch

10

Ten tiny turtles wearing T-shirts that match